S0-AAM-021

from Aunt Sue

TOM THUMB

Pictures by T. IZAWA and S. HIJIKATA

GROSSET & DUNLAP • Publishers • NEW YORK

A NATIONAL GENERAL COMPANY

There once lived a farmer and his wife who had all they wanted except a child of their own.

"If we only had a son," sighed the wife, "I would be content, even if he were no bigger than my thumb."

In time, their wish came true—they were blessed with a fine baby boy who was no bigger than the wife's thumb. "Tom Thumb" became his name.

One day the farmer went deep into the forest to chop wood. As he left the house, he spoke aloud. "If only I had someone to bring my horse and cart to me, I could haul the wood back to-night," he said.

Library of Congress Catalog Card Number: 78-157678
ISBN: 0-448-04276-2 (Trade Edition)
Illustrations Copyright © 1971 by Tadasu Izawa and Shigemi Hijikata
through management of Dairisha, Inc. Printed and bound in Japan
by Zokeisha Publications, Ltd., Roppongi, Minato-ku, Tokyo.

Once the farmer was out of sight, Tom asked his mother to hitch the horse to the cart. Then, seating himself in the horse's ear, Tom told the horse exactly which way to go. Later that day, to the farmer's great surprise, his horse appeared, pulling the cart, but with no driver!

"Here I am, Father!" called Tom. "I have brought the cart, as you wished."

Now two wicked men had seen what Tom had done and at
once began to think that they could gain much money by showing
off the tiny boy at fairs. They offered the farmer a great deal of
money for Tom. The father naturally refused, but Tom, hiding
in his father's jacket, told him to agree, assuring his father that he
would soon be home again. And so it was that Tom set out with
the two men, riding on the hatbrim of one of them so that he
could see the countryside as they traveled along.

When evening came, Tom called out, "Please, sirs, set me down. I am tired of riding up here." But as soon as the men had done this, Tom skipped off into the tall grass and disappeared down a mousehole.

The men were furious, but in the dark they could not find any trace of the boy, and so at last they lay down to rest for the night, grumbling at their bad luck. Once they were asleep, Tom crept out and, finding a snail shell under a fat toadstool, crawled in and was soon fast asleep.

The next morning he overheard the same two men discussing a robbery. "The squire has plenty of gold in his house," said one. "If only we could get in . . ."

"I can help you," called Tom.

The men were startled to hear his voice so close by and even more to discover tiny Tom in the snail shell. "How can YOU help us?" they asked, relieved to have found him once again.

"I'll slip in through the bars of the window and pass out to you whatever you want," replied Tom. And so it was agreed.

Off went the three to the squire's house. But no sooner was Tom inside than he called out in a loud voice. "What would you like me to hand to you first?"

"Hush!" cried the robbers. "You'll wake everyone!"

"I can't hear you!" shouted Tom, even louder than before. "Do you want me to pass out all the gold and silver to you?"

By this time the housemaid had been awakened from her sleep. Hearing the commotion, she soon guessed that thieves must be about, bent on stealing the squire's treasure.

Hopping out of bed, she dashed to the door and drove off the two men with a broom. Tom, being a clever boy, quietly slipped out of the house and crept away to the barn.

Early in the morning, the maid came to the barn to feed the cow. Before Tom Thumb could open his eyes, the maid had picked him up in a forkful of hay and the cow had swallowed him. He began to shout, "No more food, no more food!" and the maid thought the cow was bewitched.

The maid screamed for the squire, who came running. When

he heard "No more food!" from the cow's mouth, he turned the cow out to pasture. Tom Thumb was able to slip out of the cow's mouth unnoticed. Once more he set out to find his way home. And because of his earlier ride atop the man's hat, he had no trouble in knowing which way to go.

But he soon grew tired and stopped to rest in the shade of a leaf. At that very moment a hungry wolf happened along and swallowed the boy in one gulp. Tom, however, did not lose courage. From the wolf's stomach he told the wolf that he knew of a place where a really fine meal could be found.

The greedy wolf was quite happy to follow Tom's directions, and in a short time he trotted up to the house of Tom Thumb's parents. Knowing that the farmer and his wife would be asleep, Tom told the wolf to creep in through a hidden opening.

Once inside the house, the wolf ate all the food in the pantry.
Having eaten his fill, the wolf turned to crawl out again. But
now he had grown too fat to squeeze through the opening! Tom
called out loudly for help. The wolf struggled to escape, but by
this time the farmer had come out to the pantry to see what all the
noise was about.

"Father! Save me!" cried Tom. "I'm here in the wolf's stomach."

In an instant the farmer felled the wolf and rescued his tiny son.

Then what a wonderful time they had together as Tom told of his adventures! His mother soon had him dressed in a fine new suit of clothes, and all three lived quite comfortably and happily for many, many years.